NGOZI UKA

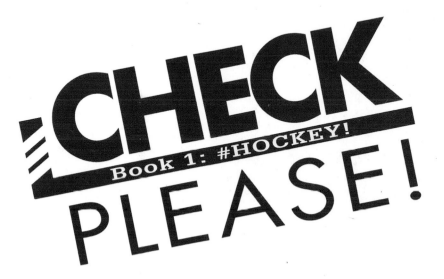

CHECK

Book 1: #HOCKEY!

PLEASE!

:01

First Second
New York

TABLE OF CONTENTS

FOREWORD

FOR A SCREENPLAY-WRITING SEMINAR during my senior year of college, I had every intention of creating some Very Serious Art™. You know—something dramatic, important, critical of various institutions, and obviously very gritty. So, enter *Hardy*, a 120-page screenplay about a hockey player who tragically falls for his best friend—a dude.

But being a Texan, a woman, and a first-generation Nigerian, I knew that writing about a white, Boston-born hockey bro would require weeks of intense anthropological study. (For starters, I could barely ice skate!) So I checked out books on hockey, attended every Yale hockey game, interviewed hockey players, their roommates, and their girlfriends, and immersed myself in the world of bro-dom. And when I emerged, not only was *Hardy* done (and surprise, it wasn't very serious art at all—it had, like, three fart jokes) but I had suffered an unintended side effect.

I had become obsessed with hockey.

The minute I began research, hockey suddenly transformed into this fast-paced, explosive, wild, and beautiful game, with a culture filled with strange rituals and cute nicknames and intense yet stoic men and women who strap knives to their boots and chase around slabs of vulcanized rubber. I had uncovered something weird and exciting and I had to tell the world. I still wanted to create, but this time something lighter and fun and much less serious. And that's how *Check, Please!* began.

The graphic novel you're about to read is a love letter to college hockey, the bonds you form in undergrad, and self-acceptance. And in a way, Eric "Bitty" Bittle is my answer to Hardy. Bitty just wants to bake, vlog, listen to pop music, and eventually learn to love himself (even if he doesn't know it yet). I don't consider this comic Very Serious Art™ at all, but I do consider it to be something even better: fun. Whether you love baking or hockey or neither or both, I hope you have fun reading Bitty's story.

Thanks, y'all!

NGOZI!

FRESHMAN YEAR

1

MEET ERIC BITTLE

29 HOURS LATER.

2

MEET THE BOYS

3

THE COACHES

4

THE HAUS

5

BAD BOB ZIMMERMANN

SO AFTER TEN SECONDS OF GOOGLING I FOUND THIS: IT'S JACK'S DAD HOISTING THE STANLEY CUP FOR THE THIRD TIME IN 1978 WITH THE MONTREAL CANADIENS.

AND THIS IS BAD BOB'S SON JACK POOPING IN THE STANLEY CUP IN 1991 WITH THE PITTSBURGH PENGUINS.

JACK'S THE ONLY PERSON IN THE NHL'S HISTORY TO HAVE DONE THAT MORE THAN ONCE. THE POOPING, THAT IS.

6

THE HOCKEY PRINCE

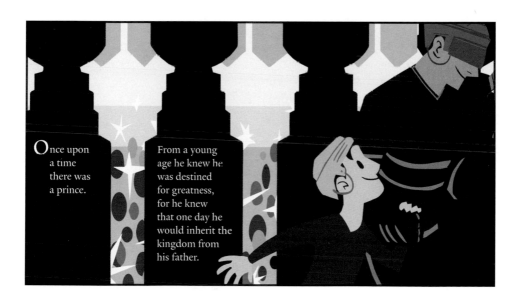

Once upon a time there was a prince.

From a young age he knew he was destined for greatness, for he knew that one day he would inherit the kingdom from his father.

So completely frightened of not being as good a king as his father, that he would stay up every night braced with the fear of mediocrity.

But the prince also had a secret.

He was scared of failure.

Terrified of it.

And so the prince took a medicine to calm his anxiety...

And he took more...

And he slew trolls!

And he slew dragons!

...But one day he took too much.

And nearly lost everything.

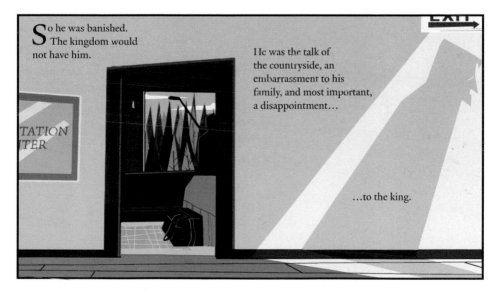

So he was banished. The kingdom would not have him.

He was the talk of the countryside, an embarrassment to his family, and most important, a disappointment…

…to the king.

But the prince would concoct a plan. He would venture back to the land of the queen. There, he would reclaim greatness…

And thereby gain entrance to the kingdom.

And all was going well. Until, of course—

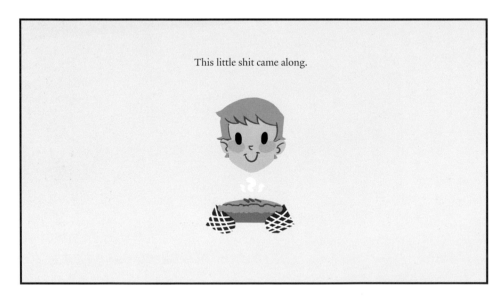

This little shit came along.

7

ASSIST!

8

CHECKING CLINIC

9

FAMILY WEEKEND

ANYWAY, THAT'S THE FAMILY SECTION DOWN THERE. JUSTIN AND ADAM'S PARENTS ARE GOING TO BE HERE, SO YOU CAN SIT WITH THEM.

OH! WILL BOB ZIMMERMANN BE THERE? DOES HE HAVE A SPOT WHERE HE USUALLY SITS? AND DON'T YOU THINK HIS SON LOOKS JUST LIKE HIM?

MOTHER, IF YOU TELL *ANYONE* YOU WERE GOOGLING JACK AND HIS DAD *I WILL HAVE A CONNIPTION.*

DICKY, YOU HAVE NO IDEA. WAY BACK WHEN, YOUR AUNT CONNIE HAD ALL HIS LITTLE CARDS EVEN THOUGH SHE'D NEVER SEEN A HOCKEY GAME. HE WAS LIKE ALL THE JONAS BROTHERS ROLLED INTO ONE WITH A SLICE OF TIM TEBOW.

(EW.)

I WANT A PICTURE DOWN THE STAIRS. COME ON.

I'M ALREADY NERVOUS ABOUT YOU WATCHING ME PLAY. I DON'T WANT TO WORRY ABOUT YOU TALKING UP BOB ZIMMERMANN LIKE IT'S SUNDAY AFTER CHURCH.

I'M NERVOUS ABOUT WATCHING *YOU!* ARE YOU SURE YOU'RE NOT GOING TO GET RUN OVER? I LOOKED AT THAT ROSTER, SOME OF THOSE BOYS ARE *BIG.* YOU'RE 5'7".

5'6" AND A HALF AND I BLAME THAT ON YOUR GENES.

WELL, I'VE BEEN GETTING HELP WITH THE CHECKING. FROM, UM...ONE OF THE GUYS ON THE TEAM.

PLUS, IT'S MY THIRD GAME. I HAVEN'T FAINTED YET.

10

SAMWELL VS. YALE — I

11

SAMWELL VS. YALE — II

12

SAMWELL VS. YALE — III

I GOTTA SAY—I WAS *A BIT WORRIED* WHEN I FIRST SAW YOU COME OUT ON THE ICE, BUT I GUESS BIG SURPRISES REALLY DO COME IN SMALL PACKAGES. THAT WAS A *CLUTCH SHOT*, SON.

WOW! UM. THANK YOU, SIR. I STILL CAN'T BELIEVE IT HAPPENED.

AND TO BE HONEST, I'M ALWAYS SO SCARED OUT THERE—I PRACTICALLY TOOK THE SHOT WITH *MY EYES CLOSED*.

A GOOD BOUNCE IS A GOOD BOUNCE. THOUGH I KNOW JACK HERE PROBABLY WANTED TO MAKE THAT GAME WINNER HIMSELF, HUH?

...

AND YOU MUST BE VERY PROUD OF YOUR SON, MRS. BITTLE.

SUZANNE. SO PROUD. BUT ERIC IS LUCKY TO GET TO PLAY WITH JACK.

YOU KNOW, COACH HALL SHOULD TRY THEM OUT ON THE SAME LINE—

I WAS JUST SAYING THE SAME THING TO ERIC. WOULDN'T THEY WORK WELL TOGETHER?

DAD, I'M GOING TO GO SHOWER UP.

IT'S A PLEASURE MEETING YOU, MRS. BITTLE.

13

THE CLOSET STORY — I

14

THE CLOSET STORY — II

LARDO

16

LINEMATES

ALL RIGHT, BOYS!

TONIGHT WE'RE ABOUT SPEED. WE'LL SEE THESE GUYS AGAIN IN THE PLAYOFFS AND THEY LIKE TO HIT HARD—BUT WE'RE THE FASTER TEAM HERE. *WE'RE BETTER.*

RIGHT. WE GOT JOHNSON STARTING IN THE NET, OLURANSI, BIRKHOLTZ, EINHARDT, ZIMMERMANN...

...AND BITTLE.

OKAY, BOYS— LET'S GET A GOOD START RIGHT OFF THE FIRST SHIFT.

17

TADPOLES

18

PLAYOFFS — I

THERE'S WATCHING JACK PLAY AND THEN THERE'S PLAYING WITH HIM.

ALL I HAVE TO DO IS GIVE HIM THE PUCK AND THEN HE JUST GOES...

BITTLE!

AND IT'S KIND OF INCREDIBLE.

ALL RIGHT, BOYS, A TOAST TO THIS FUCKING BEAUT RIGHT HERE, *JACK ZIMMERMANN*. FOR A 'SWAWESOME HATTY IN THE CLUTCHEST OF MOMENTS.

FUCKING CHEERS.

YOU'RE HAVING A BEER? RANSOM AND HOLSTER SAID YOU DIDN'T DRINK!

THEY DID? *HUH*. WELL, NOT OFTEN. AND DEFINITELY NOT AT HAUS PARTIES.

19

PLAYOFFS — II

...

20

PLAYOFFS — III

21

BANQUET

22

GOODBYE FOR THE SUMMER

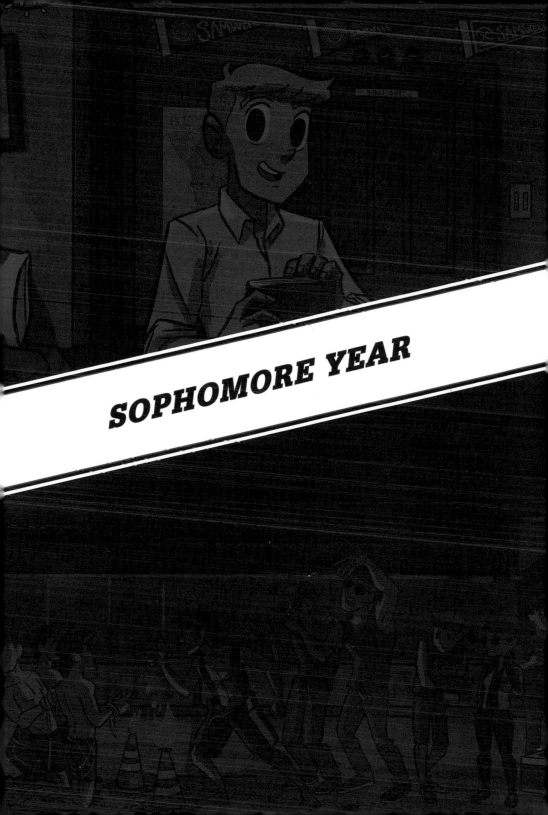

SOPHOMORE YEAR

1

MOVED IN

2

SQUARE ONE

3

MEET THE FROGS

4

HAZEAPALOOZA

FROGS, THIS EVENING YOU PARTAKE IN THE MOST SACRED OF HOCKEY RITUALS.

HAZEAPALOOZA— BEFORE IT HAZESTOCK— BONDS US IN THE SAMWELL BROTHERHOOD.

TONIGHT, YOU FROGS WILL CRAWL ONTO THE SHORES OF MANHOOD NAKED, BLINDFOLDED, AND BITCH-ASS SHITFACED.

BUT NOT ALONE!

FOR I LEARNED *ONLY HOURS AGO* THAT AMONG US, THERE WAS ONE WHO HAS YET TO ENDURE THE GAUNTLET.

JACK LAURENT ZIMMERMANN!

CAPTAIN OF OUR OWN SAMWELL MEN'S HOCKEY TEAM.

UH. I WAS... OUT OF TOWN?

5

PROVIDENCE FALCONERS

I BAKE HIM WHATEVER HE WANTS, NO QUESTIONS ASKED.

FUCK. FUCK LSATS, JDS, JD/PHDS, ALL OTHER ABBREVIATIONS, AND THE PRINCETON REVIEW'S TOP TEN LAW SCHOOLS IN GENERAL.

OH DEAR.

WHEN JACK'S NOT AT THE GYM OR THE RINK OR IN CLASS, HE'S TALKING TO HIS DAD OR HIS AGENT...

...AND TALKING CONTRACTS THAT END WITH A LOT OF O's.

OKAY, FINE—WHO *CARES* ABOUT JACK AND SHITTY, RIGHT?

YOU WATCH THIS VLOG FOR DAZZLING RECIPES AND TO FIND OUT IF I'M STILL ON THE SAMWELL MEN'S HOCKEY TEAM.

WELL, I AM, AND I'M GETTING BETTER.

I'M BY NO MEANS *FIRST-LINE MATERIAL* BUT I DID SURVIVE THAT SCRUM AT OUR GAME AGAINST QUINNIPIAC.

...THAT'S SOMETHING, RIGHT?

6

WGSS120/HIST376:
WOMEN, FOOD, AND AMERICAN CULTURE

7

PARSE — I

8

PARSE — II

9

PARSE — III

10

SHINNY

"...I'M TELLING YOU, WE CAN MAKE A PLAY OUTTA THAT."

UM, JACK?

OH. HEY, BITTLE.

THAT *DAILY* REPORTER DIDN'T ROPE YOU INTO AN INTERVIEW AFTER THAT JUMP?

OH, WELL—NO... BUT I'M GLAD I CAUGHT YOU. I JUST WANTED TO...NOT *CHECK IN--*

I'M SORRY IF I'M OVERSTEPPING— BUT I FELT THE END OF THE SEMESTER MIGHT NOT HAVE BEEN, WELL...VERY. EPIC. FOR YOU.

HAH...THANKS, BITTLE. BUT IT'S FINE.

...OKAY.

÷SIGH÷BITTLE. KENT AND I BOTH OWE EACH OTHER A LOT OF APOLOGIES.

I'M NOT PROUD OF—HE AND I...WE'VE HAD OUR DIFFERENCES.

OKAY... *OKAY.*

AND I DIDN'T MEAN TO *PRY.* YOU JUST SEEMED A LIL TENSE—

...OH? SHITTY DIDN'T WARN YOU? APPARENTLY I HAVE "MODES" OR SOMETHING.

...LIKE A ROBOT.

11

JUNIOR SHOW

12

POST I: ROADIE

13

POST II: FROZEN FOUR

"FEW EXPECTED THIS LITTLE SCHOOL FROM MASSACHUSETTS TO RETURN FOR YET ANOTHER FROZEN FOUR APPEARANCE...

"...BUT SAMWELL UNIVERSITY IS *YET AGAIN* IN THE NCAA CHAMPIONSHIPS AFTER AN UNBELIEVABLE RUN THROUGH THE PLAYOFFS."

"AND AMID RUMORS OF CONTRACTS WITH SEVERAL NHL TEAMS, ALL EYES ARE ON SENIOR CAPTAIN **JACK ZIMMERMANN**.

"IN HIS THIRD AND **FINAL YEAR** AS CAPTAIN, ZIMMERMANN SAYS HE WANTS NOTHING MORE THAN TO BRING SAMWELL ITS FIRST NATIONAL TITLE.

"IF YOU'RE A FAN OF SAMWELL, YOU KNOW THAT THERE'S A **SPARK** IN THIS TEAM THAT WASN'T THERE LAST YEAR—

"—AND IT MAY VERY WELL MAKE ALL THE DIFFERENCE.

"BUT WITH ONE GAME LEFT, ONE QUESTION REMAINS.

14

POST III: LAST GAME

15

"A"

16

KISS THE ICE

HEEEY, Y'ALL! LONG TIME NO VLOG!

CLASS DAY FOR THE SENIORS IS TOMORROW AND I REALLY SHOULD BE PACKING, BUT ONE QUICK POST BEFORE I HAVE TO RUN OFF—

I KNOW I HAVEN'T TALKED MUCH SINCE THE CHAMPIONSHIP—WHICH WAS A VERY HARD LOSS FOR US. *BUT!* SINCE THEN, SPRING SEMESTER WAS ITS TYPICAL WHIRLWIND.

RANS AND HOLTZY GOT SELECTED AS *CO-CAPTAINS* AND ARE GONNA GET THOSE "A's" ON THEIR SWEATERS NEXT SEASON, LARDO AND CHOWDER ARE FIXING TO MOVE IN SINCE THEY GOT TAPPED FOR *DIBS*—

Y'ALL, I'M TECHNICALLY A JUNIOR. THERE'S A LOT TO CATCH YOU UP ON.

THE FIRST BIG EVENT CAME RIGHT AFTER PLAYOFFS.

THOSE WHO HAD BEARDS SHAVED. OTHERS WERE A BIT MORE **DRASTIC**.

LARDS.

'SUP, SHITS?

MY SHITTY GRANDPARENTS ARE COMING TO GRADUATION, NO PUN IN-FUCKING-TENDED.

IT WAS NO FLOW OR NO GO. I JUST SKYPE-PROMISED MY MOM. **FUCK IT!**

GIMME THE CHOP!

UH.

OKAY.

AFTER THAT, WE HAD TO HELP A FRIEND FIGURE OUT HIS FUTURE.

I MEAN, SEATTLE'S FANBASE IS *DECE*. BUT NOWHERE NEAR WHAT THE FALCS HAVE.

AND DIDN'T YOU RANK LOCATION PRETTY HIGH? THAT'S AWFUL FAR.

YOU ALSO RANKED ICE TIME AND TEAM FEEL REALLY HIGH, BUT **BRAH**, IF YOU'RE GOING EXPANSION, I'D STILL LEAN TOWARD MORE CAP SPACE.

DUDE, TOTALLY HONEST? WHEN IT'S ICE TIME VERSUS CASH, A FEW HUNDY K DOESN'T MATTER TO YOU, RIGHT?

...WELL. (NOT REALLY.)

('SWAWESOME.)

SICK, THEN EXCEL'S TELLING ME SEATTLE AND BOSTON ARE SUPER OUT.

BRAH. WHY'D I HAVE TO FIND OUT FROM NHL.COM THAT YOU JUST SIGNED WITH PROVIDENCE?

OH.

I WOULD'VE TOLD YOU SOONER BUT.

I HAD A LECTURE.

WITH JACK SIGNING, THE SENIORS GRADUATING SUDDENLY BECAME TOO REAL... ÷SIGH÷

AND THEN Y'ALL OF COURSE HEARD ALL ABOUT MY TRIALS AND TRIBULATIONS WITH THE PASSING OF BETSY.

OH, BETSY ISN'T A PERSON— SHE'S THAT OLD WORKHORSE OF AN OVEN THAT I DROVE TO AN *EARLY GRAVE.*

(BLESS HER HEART.)

...YOU CAN ACTUALLY TELL WHAT'S WRONG WITH IT?

...WELL, YEAH.

AND *SORRY*, BITTY. IF SOMEONE BROUGHT THIS INTO MY UNCLE'S SHOP WE'D PROBABLY SUGGEST SELLING HER FOR SCRAP.

...OH LORD. AND TO THINK THE LAST THING I MADE IN HER WAS *BAGEL BITES.*

IF ONLY I'D KNOWN.

BUT Y'ALL KNOW WHAT? SHAME ON ME FOR FORGETTING SAMWELL HOCKEY'S NUMBER ONE MOTTO.

I WAS THINKING... SINCE BITTLE'S OVEN IS BROKEN.

WE SHOULD GET HIM A NEW ONE.

YOU KNOW, GET EVERYONE TO PITCH IN?

HIS BIRTHDAY *IS* COMING UP.

OH!!! IT CAN BE A *SURPRISE!*

PFT. A BAJILLION PERCENT ODDS HE'LL CRY.

YEAH, LEAST WE COULD DO, EH?

DEFINITELY. BASED ON ALL THE FOOD WE EAT THAT BITTY MAKES?

EXCEL SAYS WE OWE HIM, LIKE, THREE OVENS.

BUT SEE Y'ALL LATER! IT'S TIME I TAKE PART IN JACK AND SHITTY'S LAST NIGHT AS WELLIES...

KRK!

THE RITUAL OF *KISSING CENTER ICE* AT FABER DATES BACK DECADES.

BEFORE WE SENIORS LEAVE THIS HALLOWED GROUND, IT'S ONLY RIGHT FOR US TO GIVE THANKS.

SHOULD I GO FIRST?

HURRY IT UP—WE WANNA GO ON THE ROOF.

CHRIST—GIVE US ONE *FUCKING* MOMENT, WILL YOU?!?!

17

GRADUATION

...BUT IT'S EVEN HARDER TELLING PEOPLE HOW IMPORTANT THEY ARE TO YOU.

OH, IT USED TO BE A *HUGE* TRADITION. RIGHT AFTER WE TOSSED UP OUR MORTARBOARDS, ME, MY SUITEMATES, AND HALF THE CLASS? ALL IN THE POND.

RIGHT! AND JACK WAS SAYING THE TEAM WENT OUT ON THE "POND" FOR A FEW PRACTICES THIS WINTER.

IT'S WHAT MAKES SAMWELL, SAMWELL.

OH! THOSE BELLS? THAT'S THE CARILLONNEURS UP IN FOUNDER'S...

YOU'RE STILL HANGING AROUND?

OR DIDN'T WE POST ENOUGH "SELFIES"?

18

GOODBYE FOR THE SUMMER — I

19

GOODBYE FOR THE SUMMER — II

TO BE CONTINUED IN...

CHECK
Book 2: Sticks and Scones
PLEASE!

EXTRA COMICS

HOCKEY SHIT

with RANSOM $\frac{1}{3}$ Holster

flow, n.

1. the majestic mane that fluxes forth from the helmets of hockey bros. Widely considered to be the most glorious of all athletic 'dos.

SWEET FLOW CAN NOT ONLY DRASTICALLY IMPROVE ON-ICE PERFORMANCE—

chirp, v.

1. to dispatch the competition with witticisms that lower esteem, assert dominance, and put benders in place.

   Quite simply—to talk smack.

nicknames, n.

1. the noble titles hockey bros give to other hockey bros, representing trust and brotherhood. A hockey player learns a teammate's first name from his gravestone.

1. Take a syllable from your last (or first) name.
2. Add one of the following:

-ie	-zy
-y	-er
-sy	-s

3. **'Swawesome!** You're now the proud owner of a totally sick hockey nickname.* It's so easy, an idiot can do it! An idiot like you!

*Depending on the syllables in your name and the off-chance your name will produce a noun, results may vary from epically legendary to "Patsy."

BIRKHOLTZ = HOLSTER

OLURANSI = RANSOM

BITTLE = BITTY

??? = SHITTY

...LONG STORY.

AAAAND JACK DOESN'T GET ONE BECAUSE HE'S LAME.

EXCEPTION TO THE RULE!

HI!

ACTUALLY IT'S NOT THAT LONG—

WAIT... ARE YOU GUYS...FILMING SOMETHING IN HERE?

LAME!!

WARNING! DO NOT TRY THIS IN OTHER SPORTS!

OTHER ATHLETES MAY VIEW THE PRACTICE OF NICKNAMING TEAMMATES AS "CUTESY" OR "UNCOOL," OR "SOME FUCKING PUNKASS PUSSY BULLSHIT."

RANSYPOO IS RIGHT.

IF YOU TRY THIS IN ANOTHER SPORT, YOU MAY JUST GET PUNCHED IN THE FACE, THROAT, AND/OR SOLAR PLEXUS.

NASHER, KOBESY'S OPEN!

AND A SUPER TECHNICAL FOUL IS CALLED FOR A PUNCH...TO THE SOLAR PLEXUS.

hockey butt, n.

1. the totally rockin' medius, maximus, and minimus gluteal muscles that are resultant of hours of hard practice and gritty shifts on the ice.

*Used to destroy enemies and attract mates.

celly, n.

1. The cathartic release of energy catalyzed by a goal. Characterized by ebullient noise-making and loosely choreographed motion. Often accompanied by hugs.

The Fist Pump

The Into-the-Glass Jump

The Glorious Fail

CELLYS ARE USUALLY TOPPED OFF WITH **GROUP HUGS**, WHICH—GIVEN THE CIRCUMSTANCES—VARY IN INTENSITY. HERE BITTY RESPONDS TO (1) A LEAD-BUILDING GOAL, (2) A GAME-KNOTTING GOAL, AND (3) A GAME-WINNER.

"NICE GOAL!"

"CLUTCH !&#$*! GOAL!"

"RAARGGGHH!!!!"

14.5

WINTER SCREW

SHITTY AND
JACK'S DIBS

TWEETS

#HOCKEY

HEY, Y'ALL! Oh my gosh, you've worked through my vlog already? Well!! I hope you aren't planning to catch up on every single post I make on social media. Honestly, I talk about everything: what I'm baking, what homework I'm not doing, the lives and goings-ons of ALL of Samwell men's hockey, #TeamBreakfast, our games, what I #OverheardAtSamwell, and sometimes my hopes and dreams! Getting through all those tweets? *Lord.* Instead of having you read all my silly thoughts on pastries and every worry I've had about a teammate, I've found the essentials. . . . Maybe Jack was right, I do tweet a lot.

Also, that tweet I have about flirting and chirping . . . pay attention to that one! 🏒✓♥

Eric Bittle @omgcheckplease · Tue, Jun 17, 2014 | 8:16 PM

Hey, y'all! Guess it's about time I started tweeting! But I feel like I'm just gonna tweet a whole bunch of pie recipes. #omgcheckplease

Eric Bittle @omgcheckplease · Tue, Jun 17, 2014 | 8:29 PM

I do love being at home, but Madison, GA can be a bit of a hot mess during these June months. How I miss the breeze off the Samwell River!

Eric Bittle @omgcheckplease · Tue, Jun 17, 2014 | 8:32 PM

And if it weren't obvious, I love being at home because of my kitchen. <3 <3 <3 Which makes me wonder how things at the Haus are going...

Eric Bittle @omgcheckplease · Mon, Jun 23, 2014 | 9:44 PM

Skyped Shitty today; he just got back from his dad's place in Boston—apparently there's an ultimatum to get rid of his flow by graduation?

Eric Bittle @omgcheckplease · Thu, Jul 10, 2014 | 11:20 PM

Got a check-in text from Jack. What a good captain. :) It's crazy how your relationship with someone can change so much in a year.

Eric Bittle @omgcheckplease · Tue, Jul 15, 2014 | 1:27 PM

FB chat w\ Chowder today: "lol those mini pies were great!! do you think you'll bake a lot when we get back to samwell?" oh, you sweet child.

Eric Bittle @omgcheckplease · Wed, Jul 16, 2014 | 12:50 PM

ANYWAY I mention all this since I'm making a maple sugar crusted apple pie for Our Dear Captain's B-day & am testing out a recipe tonight!!!

Eric Bittle @omgcheckplease · Tue, Jul 29, 2014 | 2:30 PM

THE SAMWELL 2014–2015 COURSE SCHEDULE IS OUT!! brb looking for courses about food \(~o~)/

Eric Bittle @omgcheckplease · Tue, Jul 29, 2014 | 2:45 PM
LARDO TEXT: "Bitty! WGSS120/HIST376 . Women, Food & American Culture!!" HOLY FUCKING SHIT.

Eric Bittle @omgcheckplease · Tue, Jul 29, 2014 | 9:32 PM
...So seniors get priority for 300-level history classes. I asked the boys via group text. The only class on food taught at Samwell. T_T

Eric Bittle @omgcheckplease · Tue, Jul 29, 2014 | 9:40 PM
I have to get in that class. I'm not above playing dirty. I'll bake a bribery pie. Wouldn't be my first.

Eric Bittle @omgcheckplease · Tue, Aug 5, 2014 | 7:04 PM
Please don't scare the freshmen. We can't make new ones.

Eric Bittle @omgcheckplease · Tue, Aug 5, 2014 | 7:08 PM
I worry immensely about my adopted son, the sweet baby Chowder. If the frogs' 1st Haus party is anything like mine, he might actually die.

Eric Bittle @omgcheckplease · Tue, Aug 12, 2014 | 2:44 PM
Finally ready for school! #newhaircut

Eric Bittle @omgcheckplease · Wed, Aug 13, 2014 | 10:50 PM

Haus Sweet Haus. :)

Eric Bittle @omgcheckplease · Wed, Aug 13, 2014 | 10:51 PM

First (Birthday) Pie of Sophomore Year
Maple Sugar Crusted Apple Pie
#BittleBakes

Eric Bittle @omgcheckplease · Thu, Aug 14, 2014 | 3:16 PM

Those curtains? Got em today with #MamaBittle. AND we threw
SO many things away. Lord, I can pay my tuition from recycling
those beer cans.

Eric Bittle @omgcheckplease · Mon, Aug 25, 2014 | 1:01 PM

Jack just told me the coaches might move practice to a slightly diff.
time...
"Which means you could take that Food & Culture Class?" 0_0

Eric Bittle @omgcheckplease · Mon, Aug 25, 2014 | 1:05 PM

"If you even get in that is"
Don't you even play games with my heart, Jack Zimmermann.

Eric Bittle @omgcheckplease · Mon, Aug 25, 2014 | 5:06 PM

"...We're all fucking sexy. Why the FUCK are we all single?"—Shitty.
I just stress baked a rhubarb over that same thought, Mr. Knight.

Eric Bittle @omgcheckplease · Mon, Aug 25, 2014 | 5:09 PM

Shitty just asked Jack why the fuck he's single.
As of tweet, Jack is still stuttering out a convoluted response.

Eric Bittle @omgcheckplease · Mon, Aug 25, 2014 | 5:09 PM

"um" count: 6
"hockey" count: 18

Eric Bittle @omgcheckplease · Tue, Aug 26, 2014 | 1:36 PM

Jack: ...Bittle, have you been transcribing all of our conversations on your phone?
Me: No.
(Yes.)

Eric Bittle @omgcheckplease · Wed, Aug 27, 2014 | 1:26 PM

—food class update—this morning, i walked into a senior history seminar with only my bribery pie and a dream. i left victorious.

Eric Bittle @omgcheckplease · Wed, Aug 27, 2014 | 1:26 PM

Jack: I can't believe you bribed your way into my senior history seminar
Jack: are you tweeting what I'm saying

Eric Bittle @omgcheckplease · Thu, Aug 28, 2014 | 9:21 PM

I'm worried about our oven...It's stressing me out & I bake when I'm stressed but I can't bake if it's broken & i'm stressed out.

Eric Bittle @omgcheckplease · Tue, Sep 2, 2014 | 3:32 PM

DEX CAN FIX MY OVEN

Eric Bittle @omgcheckplease · Tue, Sep 2, 2014 | 3:32 PM

*OUR OVEN WHATEVER WE ALL KNOW IT'S MINE

Eric Bittle @omgcheckplease · Tue, Sep 2, 2014 | 3:34 PM

Dex: As long as there isn't anyone chirping over my shoulder, sure I think I can
IF YOU'RE ASKING ME TO KILL NURSEY
I'LL DO IT

Eric Bittle @omgcheckplease · Tue, Sep 2, 2014 | 9:22 PM

Jack: you're starting a pie now?...We have practice and then Food Seminar in the morning.
Me: Why're you still surprised by my behavior?

Eric Bittle @omgcheckplease · Tue, Sep 2, 2014 | 9:26 PM

Jack just asked if I vlog about him.

Eric Bittle @omgcheckplease · Tue, Sep 2, 2014 | 9:28 PM

Hm. I don't know why I tweet and vlog about my teammates so much. I mean, people find it interesting. It's like an open diary.

Eric Bittle @omgcheckplease · Tue, Sep 2, 2014 | 9:30 PM

"When you get YouTube famous don't go out and chirp me all over the internet, eh? 'Night."

Eric Bittle @omgcheckplease · Wed, Sep 3, 2014 | 8:41 AM

OMFG I think the girl sitting across from us tried to take a picture of Jack on her phone. #LordHelpUs #WGSS120

Eric Bittle @omgcheckplease · Wed, Sep 3, 2014 | 8:48 AM

Phone Girl, please, you're not even being subtle. Try Tortoise Shell Glasses Girl's approach instead: blatantly staring at Jack dreamily.

Eric Bittle @omgcheckplease · Wed, Sep 3, 2014 | 3:31 PM

"The Haus is closer to my bio seminar than the dining halls..."
Chowder stopped by just to see if I had baked anything. U_U

Eric Bittle @omgcheckplease · Wed, Sep 3, 2014 | 3:31 PM

"Bitty, when do you ever do homework?" Shut up and eat the damn pie.

Eric Bittle @omgcheckplease · Thu, Sep 4, 2014 | 10:06 AM

Why do I have class on a national holiday. #HappyBirthdayBeyonce

Eric Bittle @omgcheckplease · Thu, Sep 4, 2014 | 2:40 PM

Jack's thoughts on our Food Seminar: "Uuuh. I like it. It's interesting stuff. Yeah." Ladies and gentlemen he can hardly contain himself.

Eric Bittle @omgcheckplease · Sun, Sep 7, 2014 | 4:53 PM

Sorry...I was thinking about people leaving Samwell... Shitty has a bad habit of walking into rooms & going "OH BALLS, I'M GRADUATING."

Eric Bittle @omgcheckplease · Thu, Sep 11, 2014 | 9:44 AM

Nursey & Dex are mature, intelligent young men. Yet when together: "stop it" "I'm not even touching you" "I said—NURSEY" "OW QUIT" "BITTY"

Eric Bittle @omgcheckplease · Thu, Sep 11, 2014 | 9:49 AM

And Chowder tries to interject but he's too nice and usually just gets hit in the face. Pray for these frogs, y'all.

Eric Bittle @omgcheckplease · Sun, Sep 14, 2014 | 2:01 PM

Ha ha—have you ever accidentally called a teammate sweetheart <_<

Eric Bittle @omgcheckplease · Sun, Sep 14, 2014 | 2:03 PM

I was brave enough to say I did it? But I'm not brave enough to say to whom I did it? ~_~

Eric Bittle @omgcheckplease · Wed, Sep 17, 2014 | 2:17 PM

Jack wants to start checking practice with me again. I already got hit really bad...why can't I just avoid checks until I graduate. ;~;

Eric Bittle @omgcheckplease · Fri, Sep 19, 2014 | 10:29 AM

Jack on the phone w/ his dad a while ago: french french french I'm with Bittle french french Bittle ha ha french french no...okay, bye. ._.?

Eric Bittle @omgcheckplease · Sat, Sep 20, 2014 | 3:07 PM

My newborn goalie lamb Chowder came by looking for cookies. I started a batch right away.

Eric Bittle @omgcheckplease · Sat, Sep 20, 2014 | 3:16 PM

"You know, people just give me stuff all the time? Dex gave me his jacket today because I said it was chilly." 0_0 He's just using me.

Eric Bittle @omgcheckplease · Sat, Sep 20, 2014 | 4:36 PM
Jack: how many of those tweets do you start with "oh my god y'all"?
He thinks he's so funny.

Eric Bittle @omgcheckplease · Sat, Sep 20, 2014 | 5:15 PM
Me: I'll stop tweeting when you quit teasing me
Jack: I guess you'll never stop tweeting
(This one.)

Eric Bittle @omgcheckplease · Sun, Sep 21, 2014 | 1:42 PM
Y'all...I'm still sore from getting checked a million times at 4 in the morning.U_U...Jack doesn't think it's early. –_–

Eric Bittle @omgcheckplease · Sun, Sep 21, 2014 | 9:09 PM
I mean...I guess he doesn't have to help me...and I am getting better....

Eric Bittle @omgcheckplease · Mon, Sep 22, 2014 | 1:15 PM
I don't have *time* to date. My life's already filled up w/ school, hockey, baking, running a vlog & keeping these poor freshmen alive.

Eric Bittle @omgcheckplease · Mon, Sep 22, 2014 | 1:19 PM
Crushes are stressful. Dating is disappointing. Every relationship, you either break up or get married & then divorced. Pies can't hurt you.

Eric Bittle @omgcheckplease · Mon, Sep 22, 2014 | 1:24 PM
...And then parents. "I'm sure you'll find a nice girl up there." >_<

Eric Bittle @omgcheckplease · Tue, Sep 23, 2014 | 7:36 PM
Sitting in the Norris library with Jack. Trying to do an essay response for food class...and why am I tweeting under the table.

Eric Bittle @omgcheckplease · Tue, Sep 23, 2014 | 7:45 PM
oh god, so Jack just went to use the bathroom and tossed a note on my laptop. Yes I'm live-tweeting this; my life is not exciting.

Eric Bittle @omgcheckplease · Tue, Sep 23, 2014 | 7:46 PM

it's in french OF COURSE. the girl in the corner of this reading room is looking at me like I'm an idiot. sorry, i'm giggling this is so stupid.

Eric Bittle @omgcheckplease · Tue, Sep 23, 2014 | 7:50 PM

translation: "write your essay response" oh Lord.

Eric Bittle @omgcheckplease · Tue, Sep 23, 2014 | 7:52 PM

Okay, he's back. I left a note on his backpack. I've never seen Jack have to stifle a laugh before. #NoteGameStrong

Eric Bittle @omgcheckplease · Fri, Oct 3, 2014 | 5:38 PM

Out on Lake Quad. Talking to Lardo about boys.

Eric Bittle @omgcheckplease · Fri, Oct 3, 2014 | 5:40 PM

Lardo: Boys are dumb.
Me: It's true; we are.
Lardo: Aren't I like, super eloquent.
Me: You're succinct and I like that.

Eric Bittle @omgcheckplease · Fri, Oct 3, 2014 | 10:30 PM

You know how all people wear pants most of the time? Shitty's not most people all of the time.

Eric Bittle @omgcheckplease · Sat, Oct 4, 2014 | 8:04 PM

Going to get froyo with a slightly baked Shitty and Lardo. #SamwellSuperBerry

Eric Bittle @omgcheckplease · Sat, Oct 4, 2014 | 8:08 PM

& Jack if Shitty can drag him out of his room. We're out on the front lawn. Shitty's yelling at us from Jack's window. "HE'S PUTTING ON PANTS."

Eric Bittle @omgcheckplease · Sat, Oct 4, 2014 | 8:15 PM

From Jack's window—
Jack: Is Bittle going? If he tweets about this I'm taking his phone.
Lardo: bro hates your tweet game, bits.

Eric Bittle @omgcheckplease · Sun, Oct 5, 2014 | 2:14 AM

how to use twitter

Eric Bittle @omgcheckplease · Sun, Oct 5, 2014 | 7:51 AM

I'm never deleting that last tweet. #youtried

Eric Bittle @omgcheckplease · Sun, Oct 12, 2014 | 6:56 PM

Looking forward to: long bus rides w/ the boys
Not looking forward to: a marked increase in bathroom humor
during long bus rides w/ the boys

Eric Bittle @omgcheckplease · Sun, Oct 12, 2014 | 6:58 PM

You'd think there'd only be so many dirty jokes. But OH no! Never
underestimate the humor of boys ages 18 to 23...And Lardo!

Eric Bittle @omgcheckplease · Tue, Oct 14, 2014 | 8:54 PM

Shitty: Dex, brah. If you grew your hair out you'd have some flamin'
flow. Sick carroty lettuce, maaaan.
Dex: I cut my hair once a month.

Eric Bittle @omgcheckplease · Wed, Oct 15, 2014 | 8:23 AM

Me: Jack! You wanna get a Pumpkin Spice Latte with me before
class? :) :) :)
Jack: You shouldn't be drinking those.
Me: :(:(:(

Eric Bittle @omgcheckplease · Wed, Oct 15, 2014 | 9:11 AM

Dragging Jack to Annie's before class. Without caffeine I am not a
southern gentleman.

Eric Bittle @omgcheckplease · Wed, Oct 15, 2014 | 9:32 AM

OMFG few things are funnier than watching Jack guess who's
playing on the radio in here. I can't breathe.

Eric Bittle @omgcheckplease · Wed, Oct 15, 2014 | 9:35 AM

TOO HARD TO TWEET. He keeps guessing TAYLOR SWIFT. HELP

Eric Bittle @omgcheckplease · Wed, Oct 15, 2014 | 9:41 AM

Jack: It's way too easy to make you laugh. Make sure you tweet that.

Eric Bittle @omgcheckplease · Fri, Oct 17, 2014 | 8:09 AM

Getting called into Coach Hall's office is like being sent to the principal...Let's get this over with...

Eric Bittle @omgcheckplease · Fri, Oct 17, 2014 | 8:12 AM

...I didn't have the best practice today. You can't throw someone off a team after one awful practice, right?...ugh.

Eric Bittle @omgcheckplease · Mon, Oct 20, 2014 | 6:50 PM

Our final for Food Class will involve creating a dish from an old recipe and thus:

Jack:...I might need your help.

>:)

Eric Bittle @omgcheckplease · Mon, Oct 20, 2014 | 9:15 PM

Chowder: we tried to get Nursey to take intro programming with us!

Dex: he said he's more of a "poetry guy."

Dex's eye roll was AUDIBLE.

Eric Bittle @omgcheckplease · Tue, Oct 21, 2014 | 10:20 AM

Chirping and flirting are variants on the same idea.

Eric Bittle @omgcheckplease · Thu, Oct 23, 2014 | 8:41 AM

Oh, okay, I think Nursey's trying to set Dex up with one of his friends from Andover for a screw date or something.

Eric Bittle @omgcheckplease · Thu, Oct 23, 2014 | 8:43 AM

Nursey: She does experimental theater & makes her own clothes. Sick, riiiight?

Chowder: wow!

Dex: That entire sentence was frustrating.

Eric Bittle @omgcheckplease · Fri, Oct 24, 2014 | 7:01 PM

Shitty: WHELP. My Last First-Game at Samwell Ever is next week.

Eric Bittle @omgcheckplease · Mon, Oct 27, 2014 | 10:05 AM

text: "stay hydrated this week"
Jack Zimmermann is a special combination of thoughtful and awkward.

Eric Bittle @omgcheckplease · Tue, Oct 28, 2014 | 9:13 AM

Hockey is important, but MUST we have a game on Halloween???
I'm gonna miss SO many trick-or-treating babies in SO many pumpkin costumes.

Eric Bittle @omgcheckplease · Fri, Oct 31, 2014 | 1:43 PM

#naptime Oh no...This is what dorms are for...
#SweetBabyChowder

Eric Bittle @omgcheckplease · Fri, Oct 31, 2014 | 2:35 PM

I swear I'm going to get rid of that couch before I graduate...it's seen the worst of humanity.

Eric Bittle @omgcheckplease · Fri, Oct 31, 2014 | 4:27 PM

Lardo: sup boys
Lardo: wreck shit tonight (^o^)/
~*best manager*~

Eric Bittle @omgcheckplease · Fri, Oct 31, 2014 | 4:49 PM

After this I'm putting away my phone. Thanks for all the support!!
#SamwellMensHockey #LetsGoBoys

Eric Bittle @omgcheckplease · Fri, Oct 31, 2014 | 9:15 PM

Samwell 3-1!! Samwell Halloween 2014!

Eric Bittle @omgcheckplease · Mon, Nov 3, 2014 | 1:07 PM

Nursey's so cool, but then he drops a whole plate of pasta on some poor bio major in the dhall and then I remember he's just a frog.

Eric Bittle @omgcheckplease · Mon, Nov 3, 2014 | 11:08 PM

I was falling asleep until Jack shouted "Shits! Sleep in your OWN BED" and then several words in French.

Eric Bittle @omgcheckplease · Mon, Nov 3, 2014 | 11:13 PM

(Shitty just shrieked "OW." Jack's laughing.)
(Oh my goodness, how are we a functioning hockey team.)

Eric Bittle @omgcheckplease · Tue, Nov 4, 2014 | 8:11 PM

At the library with The Captain.

Eric Bittle @omgcheckplease · Tue, Nov 4, 2014 | 10:02 PM

Jack: You only tweeted twice while we were working, Bittle. That's a record.
Jack's Chirp Game's Strong.

Eric Bittle @omgcheckplease · Tue, Nov 4, 2014 | 10:04 PM

(To be fair, it's hard to goof off when you're in Jack's peripheral vision.)

Eric Bittle @omgcheckplease · Tue, Nov 4, 2014 | 10:07 PM

Jack wants to walk past Faber.

Taking the long way back to the #HausSweetHaus.

Eric Bittle @omgcheckplease · Mon, Nov 10, 2014 | 8:01 PM

Things I Talk to My Father About: — My Ice Time — My Diet ("More Protein") — My Stats — If I'm feeling OK/"toughin it out" — Jack Zimmermann

Eric Bittle @omgcheckplease · Mon, Nov 10, 2014 | 8:03 PM

...You know, I should be happy. He actually cares abt something I'm doing. He's even watching more hockey & listens to WSMC for our games.

Eric Bittle @omgcheckplease · Mon, Nov 10, 2014 | 8:05 PM

And he asks about Jack because...well, my father LOVES sports. He's just as fascinated as everyone else about what team Jack'll choose.

Eric Bittle @omgcheckplease · Thu, Nov 13, 2014 | 8:28 AM

There are people who sit on Lake Quad benches? And then there's Nursey. "CHILL. Why would we neglect this obscene pile of leaves? Man."

Eric Bittle @omgcheckplease · Thu, Nov 13, 2014 | 2:50 PM

Do you ever think about being with someone but realize it's impossible and then get really sad so you bake a pie instead.

Eric Bittle @omgcheckplease · Thu, Nov 13, 2014 | 3:00 PM

(I tweet a lot abt being single, but I'm OK, really. I'm on a great team w/ all my best friends + I go to a wonderful school. I'm thankful.)

Eric Bittle @omgcheckplease · Thu, Nov 13, 2014 | 3:01 PM

(I wish I could tell high school Eric Bittle all of this. It gets so much better.)

Eric Bittle @omgcheckplease · Thu, Nov 13, 2014 | 9:21 PM

Cleaning the kitchen while listening to Jack talk about the nuances of power plays. :)

Eric Bittle @omgcheckplease · Sun, Nov 16, 2014 | 2:40 PM

Getting texts from Jack Zimmermann himself who is sitting in a room mere FEET away from mine.

Eric Bittle @omgcheckplease · Sun, Nov 16, 2014 | 2:40 PM

Jack: we need to cook for class :/

Eric Bittle @omgcheckplease · Sun, Nov 16, 2014 | 2:42 PM

Jack: we can go to stop & shop today. have a skype call with a GM @ 6. can we go before then

Eric Bittle @omgcheckplease · Sun, Nov 16, 2014 | 2:46 PM

Jack's Sunday To-Do List: (1) Negotiate Multi-Million Dollar NHL Contracts (2) Go Grocery Shopping with Bittle

Eric Bittle @omgcheckplease · Tue, Nov 25, 2014 | 6:33 PM

quick nursey or dex for a piggyback ride race!! shitty is on the other side of river quad officiating!!

Eric Bittle @omgcheckplease · Tue, Nov 25, 2014 | 6:34 PM

okay wish us luck!!!!

Eric Bittle @omgcheckplease · Tue, Nov 25, 2014 | 6:40 PM

we lost. :(

Eric Bittle @omgcheckplease · Tue, Nov 25, 2014 | 6:42 PM

BUT Dex tripped over the sidewalk and he and Chowder went careening into half the women's volleyball team i am still laughing

Eric Bittle @omgcheckplease · Tue, Nov 25, 2014 | 6:43 PM

chowder is mortified he keeps asking the same girl if she's okay (they were both in the same pile of leaves for a second there)

Eric Bittle @omgcheckplease · Tue, Nov 25, 2014 | 10:59 PM

Chowder Text: "I HAVE A DATE!!!!!!!!...(FOR SCREW!!!!!!!!)" Ransom and Holster work quickly.

Eric Bittle @omgcheckplease · Fri, Nov 28, 2014 | 1:55 AM

"Hockey players baking. My brother won't let me live this down."
So that happened. Dex w/ the asst. Happy Thanksgiving!! (Y'all!)
#Hausgiving.

Eric Bittle @omgcheckplease · Sat, Nov 29, 2014 | 9:40 AM

What is homework? What is finals? -_-! I'd like to pour one out for
my GPA this semester.

Eric Bittle @omgcheckplease · Sat, Nov 29, 2014 | 9:48 AM

Transcribing the following interaction across the hall:
Jack: get the @$% out my room SHITS
Shitty: good morning man it's 9:30 you slept in

Eric Bittle @omgcheckplease · Sat, Nov 29, 2014 | 9:59 AM

[5 min. of Jack & Shitty talking quietly]...[10 sec. of Shitty laughing
uproariously]...[3 sec. of Jack chuckling]

Eric Bittle @omgcheckplease · Tue, Dec 2, 2014 | 10:27 AM

RIP My GPA. Did y'all know I was taking a calc course this
semester? I apparently didn't either.

Eric Bittle @omgcheckplease · Tue, Dec 2, 2014 | 1:46 PM

I was freaking out to Jack about finals and he just looked at me
and said "17."

Eric Bittle @omgcheckplease · Tue, Dec 2, 2014 | 2:59 PM

Jack: That's the number of pies you baked in September. In case you were wondering where your time went. #ChirpGameStrong

Eric Bittle @omgcheckplease · Sat, Dec 6, 2014 | 11:45 PM

It's #SamwellWinterScrew. There's a lot of things I want to say right now, but it's raining, and I told my date I was going to the restroom 10 minutes ago.

Eric Bittle @omgcheckplease · Sat, Dec 6, 2014 | 11:52 PM

And though opinions vary among the #SamwellMensHockey team, let the record show: Jack Zimmermann is not a terrible dancer. #SamwellWinterScrew

Eric Bittle @omgcheckplease · Sunday, Dec 7, 2014 | 1:57 PM

Things I'll miss next year: hearing the aftermath of Shitty barging into Jack's room in the mornings.

Eric Bittle @omgcheckplease · Sunday, Dec 7, 2014 | 1:59 PM

Shitty: DEETS DEETS DEETS DEETS WINTERSCREW??
Jack: ...I have no deets, man.

Eric Bittle @omgcheckplease · Sunday, Dec 7, 2014 | 2:03 PM

Shitty: don't give me any of that dumbass zimmermanns don't kiss and tell bullshit.
Jack: get out. OF MY BED

Eric Bittle @omgcheckplease · Sunday, Dec 7, 2014 | 2:11 PM

Shitty: no one will do this with you in the NHL
Shitty: shhhh don't fight ow ow ow
Shitty: why do you resist my snuggles

Eric Bittle @omgcheckplease · Sunday, Dec 7, 2014 | 7:06 PM

Dex's expression 60% of the time is "how do these people exist"

Eric Bittle @omgcheckplease · Sunday, Dec 7, 2014 | 9:42 PM

Ransom: it's reading week
Holster: yup gotta study
Ransom: how many kegsters can we throw
Holster: probably 9

Eric Bittle @omgcheckplease · Sunday, Dec 7, 2014 | 9:44 PM

(After I started complaining)
Ransom: My dear Bits. If you're drunk when you're studying, all you have to do is take the test drunk.

Eric Bittle @omgcheckplease · Tue, Dec 9, 2014 | 10:40 PM

Jack finished his essay for our history seminar already. HOW????

Eric Bittle @omgcheckplease · Tue, Dec 9, 2014 | 10:43 PM

Jack: I'm sure you'd be done too if you had tweeted it.
Jack: Is that an option?
Jack Zimmermann: :^)

Eric Bittle @omgcheckplease · Tue, Dec 9, 2014 | 10:47 PM

I try to prepare myself for Jack Zimmermann's chirping but I am never ready.

Eric Bittle @omgcheckplease · Tue, Dec 9, 2014 | 10:50 PM

He's so happy with himself right now. And Jack doesn't have that many expressions.

Eric Bittle @omgcheckplease · Fri, Dec 12, 2014 | 12:13 PM

I'm going to throw out that couch before I graduate.

Eric Bittle @omgcheckplease · Fri, Dec 12, 2014 | 4:38 PM

Apparently Jack is in "Procrastinate by Bothering Bittle Mode." I'm not a fan.

Eric Bittle @omgcheckplease · Fri, Dec 12, 2014 | 4:39 PM

Doesn't he have important hockey related activities to attend to???

Eric Bittle @omgcheckplease · Fri, Dec 12, 2014 | 4:42 PM

Jack: what are you blogging about
Jack: is that the camera you use
Jack: oh wow you write a script

Eric Bittle @omgcheckplease · Fri, Dec 12, 2014 | 4:44 PM

Jack: what're you texting
shows him tweets
Jack: I said "where'd you get that camera" not "is that the camera you use." Come on, Bittle.

Eric Bittle @omgcheckplease · Fri, Dec 12, 2014 | 4:46 PM

Give this boy back to Montreal.

Eric Bittle @omgcheckplease · Fri, Dec 12, 2014 | 11:25 PM

Holster: KEGSTER
Ransom: TOMORROW
Holster: THE HAUS
Ransom: WE INVITED 1000 PEOPLE ON
FACEBOOK.....#EPIKEGSTER

Eric Bittle @omgcheckplease · Fri, Dec 12, 2014 | 11:25 PM

D:...I'm just...#Terrified.

Eric Bittle @omgcheckplease · Sat, Dec 13, 2014 | 8:05 PM

Rans and Holster have an excel sheet for this kegster. I don't know
what's on it but its very existence scares me.

Eric Bittle @omgcheckplease · Sat, Dec 13, 2014 | 8:09 PM

If I do have a good time it'll be thanks to whatever Shitty and Lardo
ARE BREWING IN OUR BATHTUB.

Eric Bittle @omgcheckplease · Sat, Dec 13, 2014 | 8:10 PM

Me: what're y'all making in the tub?
Shitty: kegster punch
Me: what're y'all making the frogs do?
Lardo: kegster chores

Eric Bittle @omgcheckplease · Sat, Dec 13, 2014 | 11:05 PM

Have you ever had 40 people walk into your house at once.
#Epikegster

Eric Bittle @omgcheckplease · Sat, Dec 13, 2014 | 11:28 PM

[a wild Jack Zimmermann appears]

Eric Bittle @omgcheckplease · Sat, Dec 13, 2014 | 11:31 PM

Me: *talks to senior hockey captain so he won't be an awkward
wallflower at #Epikegster*
Senior Hockey Captain: *seems grateful*

Eric Bittle @omgcheckplease · Sat, Dec 13, 2014 | 11:51 PM

Jack: I've only experienced one #EpiKegster

Jack: it took up two issues of the Swallow

Jack: no I'm not kidding

Eric Bittle @omgcheckplease · Sun, Dec 14, 2014 | 12:14 AM

Shitty: JACK ZIMMERMANN HAVING FUN AT A COLLEGE PARTY

Shitty: IT'S AN #EPIKEGSTERMAS MIRACLE

Eric Bittle @omgcheckplease · Sun, Dec 14, 2014 | 12:28 AM

"Oh my fucking GOD that's FUCKING Kent Parson!" —Some Drunk Lax Bro at #EpiKegster (probably).

Eric Bittle @omgcheckplease · Sun, Dec 14, 2014 | 12:28 AM

No, sweetheart, that's Jack Zimmermann. #Bless...But. hmm. Should I be worried about Nursey crowdsurfing?

Eric Bittle @omgcheckplease · Sun, Dec 14, 2014 | 12:50 AM

Oh. It was Kent Parson!!

Eric Bittle @omgcheckplease · Sun, Dec 14, 2014 | 1:07 AM

lord, I'm getting starstruck

Eric Bittle @omgcheckplease · Sun, Dec 14, 2014 | 1:33 AM

Had to get a pic w/ NHL star Kent Parson!! #SamwellUniversity #TypicalSamwellParty #EpiKegster #NHL #omgcheckplease

Eric Bittle @omgcheckplease · Sun, Dec 14, 2014 | 1:33 AM

!!!! HE'S SO NICE!!!!!

Eric Bittle @omgcheckplease · Sun, Dec 14, 2014 | 1:38 AM

Where is Jack?

Eric Bittle @omgcheckplease · Sun, Dec 14, 2014 | 10:21 AM

Well, the frogs survived.

Eric Bittle @omgcheckplease · Sun, Dec 14, 2014 | 10:23 AM

(survived is being generous)
Me: good morning!
Nursey: hhhhmmmmmnnggggggrrgghhhhhhhhhhh

Eric Bittle @omgcheckplease · Mon, Dec 15, 2014 | 9:57 AM

Oh Dear God.
All of the frogs are in the Swallow.

Eric Bittle @omgcheckplease · Mon, Dec 15, 2014 | 9:59 AM

Rans:...is this what new fathers feel like? *whispers* Hashtag EpiKegster.

Eric Bittle @omgcheckplease · Mon, Dec 15, 2014 | 3:03 PM

Okay, Jack & Shitty are fixing to head out. I'm going on a very dangerous mission. Wish me luck.

Eric Bittle @omgcheckplease · Mon, Dec 15, 2014 | 3:24 PM

MISSION ACCOMPLISHED And now to wait for him to find them... [cookies!]

Eric Bittle @omgcheckplease · Tue, Dec 16, 2014 | 12:34 PM

Text from Jack: i'm surprised your cookies got through customs, Bittle
UvU He found them.

Eric Bittle @omgcheckplease · Sat, Dec 20, 2014 | 9:12 PM

Dear Santa, for Christmas I'd like my hockey butt, thank you. —ERB
(Well. My birthday's in May. Maybe I'll get it by then. :/)

Eric Bittle @omgcheckplease · Thu, Dec 25, 2014 | 11:41 AM

Merry Christmas, y'all! (^o^)/

Eric Bittle @omgcheckplease · Thu, Dec 25, 2014 | 6:06 PM

SMH Group Text:
Jack: Merry Christmas
Jack: We have a game next week.

Eric Bittle @omgcheckplease · Fri, Dec 26, 2014 | 6:08 PM

Once we get back to Samwell, which of my teammates would do squats with me every day? (a) Chowder (b) Lardo (c) Holster (d) Other

Eric Bittle @omgcheckplease · Fri, Dec 26, 2014 | 6:09 PM

Ransom: #FlyBittyBooty2015

Eric Bittle @omgcheckplease · Sun, Dec 28, 2014 | 5:14 PM

My baby-child, my son and ward, the warm ray of sunshine that is the net-minder Chris "Chowder" Chow...no longer appears to be single.

Eric Bittle @omgcheckplease · Sun, Dec 28, 2014 | 5:16 PM

Apparently he and Volleyball Girl are both from California....

Eric Bittle @omgcheckplease · Mon, Dec 29, 2014 | 10:51 PM

YES. Jack butt-texted the group TEXT. My day is made. He shouldn't've admitted to it. Rookie Mistake.

Eric Bittle @omgcheckplease · Mon, Dec 29, 2014 | 10:52 PM

My phone won't stop vibrating from the CONSTANT CHIRPING. #GotYourBack

Eric Bittle @omgcheckplease · Mon, Dec 29, 2014 | 10:52 PM

If Holster were a shark, this faux pas would be a wounded sea lion. #HolsterHasBeenWaitingForThisDay

Eric Bittle @omgcheckplease · Mon, Dec 29, 2014 | 10:58 PM

SMH Group Text:
Jack: ok haha very funny
Jack: you got me
Jack: my ass is big i get it
Holster: and it miSSES US MORE THAN you DO

Eric Bittle @omgcheckplease · Mon, Dec 29, 2014 | 11:09 PM

(What he texted:
Jack: edijdia;;;;;;;;;;;;:-):-):-):-)
Jack: :-):-)
Shitty: WHAT THE FUCK)

Eric Bittle @omgcheckplease · Fri, Jan 2, 2015 | 7:45 PM

enters Haus
immediately do squats w/ Rans
#BetterBittyBootyBureau2015

Eric Bittle @omgcheckplease · Fri, Jan 2, 2015 | 7:51 PM

"Hey, Bittle. Oh, squats. Good."
—Jack Zimmermann

Eric Bittle @omgcheckplease · Sat, Jan 3, 2015 | 12:15 PM

Chowder's reaction to coming back to Samwell: "Wow!! It's like I
never left! But I totally did because I really missed you guys!!"
#SweetBabyChowder

Eric Bittle @omgcheckplease · Sat, Jan 3, 2015 | 12:21 PM

Nursey: You miss me, Poindexter?
Dex: No.
Nursey: You're always free to skype me.

Eric Bittle @omgcheckplease · Sat, Jan 3, 2015 | 8:21 PM

"That food seminar was something, eh?"
—Jack Zimmermann

Eric Bittle @omgcheckplease · Sun, Jan 4, 2015 | 11:38 AM

Afternoon game! #LetsGoBoys

Eric Bittle @omgcheckplease · Sun, Jan 4, 2015 | 4:27 PM
Good win, even if I got banged up a little! Spears over body checks any day imho.

Eric Bittle @omgcheckplease · Mon, Jan 5, 2015 | 11:15 AM
The Psychology, Biology & Politics of Food WAS AMAZING. Ugggh, a perfect lecture class. I will take EVERY food class at Samwell!

Eric Bittle @omgcheckplease · Fri, Jan 9, 2015 | 10:12 PM
Rans:...bro. every game of words with friends can easily turn into words with enemies
Hoslter:...*bro*

Eric Bittle @omgcheckplease · Sat, Jan 10, 2015 | 5:16 PM
jack's hatty tho

Eric Bittle @omgcheckplease · Sat, Jan 10, 2015 | 7:01 PM
Dex: Jack, how often do you do that?
Jack: do what?
Jack: ...oh...you mean get hat tric-
Shitty: HE SAID IT
EVERYONE THROWS HATS AT JACK

Eric Bittle @omgcheckplease · Sat, Jan 10, 2015 | 7:02 PM
Jack Zimmermann is covered in hats and laughing. We're going to get kicked out of this restaurant. #RoadieAdventures

Eric Bittle @omgcheckplease · Thu, Jan 15, 2015 | 1:56 PM
Holster: WAIT BITS is that food lecture a science credit?
Nursey: hold up, it's a science credit???
Lardo: did someone say science credit

Eric Bittle @omgcheckplease · Thu, Jan 15, 2015 | 1:58 PM
If half this hockey team takes this class with me I'm going to be somewhat uncomfortable. I see you people EVERY DAY ALREADY.

Eric Bittle @omgcheckplease · Sun, Jan 18, 2015 | 2:12 PM
THANK GOODNESS Shitty forced me to look out the window with him. Jack is taking photos of the tree in our front yard with a DSLR.

Eric Bittle @omgcheckplease · Sun, Jan 18, 2015 | 2:20 PM

Shitty: Yaaa it's for his photography class, but I like to pretend he's going nuts. Hashtag Jack As Second-Semester Senior.

Eric Bittle @omgcheckplease · Sun, Jan 18, 2015 | 2:27 PM

He's showing Lardo his photos. I think they're talking composition. Aaaand now Shitty's shouting at him to take a picture of us.

Eric Bittle @omgcheckplease · Sun, Jan 18, 2015 | 2:32 PM

So I'm probably going to be in Jack's homework assignment.

Eric Bittle @omgcheckplease · Thu, Jan 22, 2015 | 9:31 AM

I've always baked to cope with the fact that I've been single for most of my life. (...Maybe that's why I'm good at it? Hm.)

Eric Bittle @omgcheckplease · Mon, Jan 26, 2015 | 12:14 PM

So. Blizzards, eh?

Eric Bittle @omgcheckplease · Tue, Jan 27, 2015 | 12:44 PM

"Yeeep, Bits. That's a metric shit ton of snow." —Shitty, partially clothed, looking out at our front yard, w/ a mug full of hot cocoa.

Eric Bittle @omgcheckplease · Tue, Jan 27, 2015 | 12:48 PM

Shitty: Dex is texting about Dibs for shoveling us out. Christ I love that ambitious little butt nugget.

Eric Bittle @omgcheckplease · Wed, Jan 28, 2015 | 11:59 AM

"I'm gonna go take some pictures for class," said Jack Zimmermann casually traipsing into two feet of snow.

Eric Bittle @omgcheckplease · Thu, Jan 29, 2015 | 12:20 AM

Banging on my door.
"Bittle. Team practice tomorrow afternoon."
"...I took some cool pictures today."

Eric Bittle @omgcheckplease · Thu, Jan 29, 2015 | 12:22 AM

Jack is either somber and concerned about us making playoffs? or in this...strange senior mood. That's what I'm calling it.

Eric Bittle @omgcheckplease · Thu, Jan 29, 2015 | 12:26 AM

Jack: there were some kids nordic skiing down elm street

Jack: neat eh. they didn't even see me

Eric Bittle @omgcheckplease · Thu, Jan 29, 2015 | 12:28 AM

Jack: I like that, you know? they didn't even know I was there

Eric Bittle @omgcheckplease · Sat, Jan 31, 2015 | 12:22 PM

Dex: [fixes broken chair. stops fridge door from squeaking. saves Betsy.] ;o;

Eric Bittle @omgcheckplease · Sun, Feb 1, 2015 | 2:17 PM

Ransom's doing homework in the kitchen because "Holtzy won't stop singing this STUPID Wuthering Heights song."

Eric Bittle @omgcheckplease · Sun, Feb 1, 2015 | 2:21 PM

Ransom: i have no idea how Holster's voice gets so high, like the pitch is OH WAIT BITS DO YOU NEED A DATE FOR VALENTINE'S DAY???????

Eric Bittle @omgcheckplease · Sun, Feb 1, 2015 | 2:34 PM

Shitty: what are you guys doing

Rans: finding Bitty a date

Jack: why is Bittle under the table

Eric Bittle @omgcheckplease · Sun, Feb 1, 2015 | 2:41 PM

um please do not photograph me while i'm down here.

Jack: while you're down there do you want to see some photos, Bittle?

DEAR GOD!!!!!!!!

Eric Bittle @omgcheckplease · Wed, Feb 4, 2015 | 12:26 AM

Me: [sneezes]

Jack: [across the hall] bless you

Jack: go to sleep

Jack: we have practice

Eric Bittle @omgcheckplease · Thu, Feb 5, 2015 | 2:31 PM

Me: [sees jack across River quad]
Me: [waves]
Jack: [waves]
Jack: [walks across quad]
Jack: [jumps over snowbank]
Jack: do you want coffee?

Eric Bittle @omgcheckplease · Thu, Feb 5, 2015 | 3:06 PM

Jack: oh yeah, Bittle, I wanted to show—[pulls out camera and knocks into my coffee and spills entire contents on my Samwell hoodie]

Eric Bittle @omgcheckplease · Thu, Feb 5, 2015 | 3:09 PM

what is wrong with this boy

Eric Bittle @omgcheckplease · Fri, Feb 6, 2015 | 11:50 AM

My pregame ritual involves getting pumped with my favorite playlist! Others like to get broody / eat pb&j sandwiches instead w/e.

Eric Bittle @omgcheckplease · Mon, Feb 16, 2015 | 11:41 AM

Overheard at Samwell
girl 1: half the hockey team is in the class
girl 2: ugh they would
girl 1: they're so loud

Eric Bittle @omgcheckplease · Wed, Feb 18, 2015 | 11:29 AM

"HOW? HOW can you be 'CLOSE TO DONE'???" shouts Shitty re: Jack's thesis. We're at Norris library but of course that doesn't matter.

Eric Bittle @omgcheckplease · Wed, Feb 18, 2015 | 11:31 AM

Shitty: BRAH. Where do you find TIME?
Jack:...I do a little every night?
Shitty: That's???? Not??? Real???

Eric Bittle @omgcheckplease · Wed, Feb 18, 2015 | 11:32 AM

if it isn't obvious, half of my tweets are done while cackling

Eric Bittle @omgcheckplease · Wed, Feb 18, 2015 | 11:37 AM
"I don't really procrastinate, I guess."
—Jack Zimmermann
#ThingsIWillNeverSay

 Eric Bittle @omgcheckplease · Thu, Feb 19, 2015 | 5:33 PM
When you're crossing the River and realize the guy taking pictures
of a goose is the captain of the hockey team.

 Eric Bittle @omgcheckplease · Thu, Feb 19, 2015 | 10:10 PM
:) Game tomorrow!

 Eric Bittle @omgcheckplease · Sat, Feb 21, 2015 | 10:50 AM
sigh Nursey definitely just hit a kid in the face with his hockey bag.
#MostDangerousDman #RoadieAdventures

 Eric Bittle @omgcheckplease · Sat, Feb 21, 2015 | 10:58 AM
Dear Lord, this child is like 8 and he just said, "nah, it's cool. Good
luck with your game, bro." #MoreChillThanDerekNurse

 Eric Bittle @omgcheckplease · Sat, Feb 21, 2015 | 11:07 AM
Jack: Nice check, Nurse. (All of SMH: [CACKLES])

 Eric Bittle @omgcheckplease · Tue, Feb 24, 2015 | 9:26 AM
Holster: "MEN'S HOCKEY: Wellies finish weekend w/ road sweep;
clinch ECAC playoff spot." you know sometimes the Daily isn't a
piece of crap.

 Eric Bittle @omgcheckplease · Tue, Feb 24, 2015 | 9:39 AM
Holster: "'We're a close knit group of guys. We look out for each
other on the ice,' forward and team capt. Jack Zimmermann '15
said."

 Eric Bittle @omgcheckplease · Tue, Feb 24, 2015 | 9:43 AM
Holster: Guys, Jack loves us! SAY YOU LOVE US!
Jack: I love you.
#TeamBreakfast

Eric Bittle @omgcheckplease · Thu, Feb 26, 2015 | 2:42 PM

Lardo's art show is this weekend! Excited to mingle with the art majors! I hope they like hockey players.

Eric Bittle @omgcheckplease · Thu, Feb 26, 2015 | 11:31 PM

Jack has a critique tomorrow and wants feedback on photos. It is SO past his bedtime. Also? I'm NO Lardo...

Eric Bittle @omgcheckplease · Thu, Feb 26, 2015 | 11:38 PM

Jack: I figured you'd be up baking a pie or three. (???????? I'm making TWO.)

Eric Bittle @omgcheckplease · Thu, Feb 26, 2015 | 11:58 PM

Jack: this goose one isn't dumb?
Me: no, it's charming!

Eric Bittle @omgcheckplease · Fri, Feb 27, 2015 | 12:10 AM

I did NOT ask for so many chirps this late at night

Eric Bittle @omgcheckplease · Fri, Feb 27, 2015 | 8:18 PM

Current location: Koetter Art & Student Center, right on the Pond.

Eric Bittle @omgcheckplease · Fri, Feb 27, 2015 | 8:59 PM

Have you ever heard five college hockey players earnestly trying to dissect modern art?

Eric Bittle @omgcheckplease · Fri, Feb 27, 2015 | 9:00 PM

Shitty: Ah yes, Lardo, brilliant visual metaphor this
Holster: ah yes indeed
Rans: ah yes rather indeed
Lardo: you guys are idiots

Eric Bittle @omgcheckplease · Fri, Feb 27, 2015 | 9:30 PM

!!!!!!!!!!! SHITTY GOT INTO LAW SCHOOL

Eric Bittle @omgcheckplease · Sat, Feb 28, 2015 | 1:32 AM

...late night froyo with Lardo. game tomorrow. we're gonna regret it in the morning, but I honestly couldn't care <3

Eric Bittle @omgcheckplease · Tue, Mar 3, 2015 | 11:29 PM

My teammates deserve everything. Every last one of us works so hard.

Eric Bittle @omgcheckplease · Tue, Mar 3, 2015 | 11:38 PM

For them, I couldn't bake a pie big enough. (Which sounds sweet, but seriously they're all bottomless pits.)

Eric Bittle @omgcheckplease · Sun, Mar 8, 2015 | 1:01 PM

Jack:...i probably can't do much photography when i'm playing professionally
Me: offseason, jack
Lardo: plz be that one artsy hipster NHL bro

Eric Bittle @omgcheckplease · Sat, Mar 21, 2015 | 9:04 PM

It's always #OneMoreGame.

Eric Bittle @omgcheckplease · Fri, Mar 27, 2015 | 6:25 PM

\(^o^)/ LET'S GO BOYS!

Eric Bittle @omgcheckplease · Sat, Mar 28, 2015 | 12:18 PM

Happy 22nd, Rans!

Eric Bittle @omgcheckplease · Sat, Mar 28, 2015 | 10:08 PM

we're moving on :)

Eric Bittle @omgcheckplease · Sun, Apr 5, 2015 | 11:50 PM

I'm almost done with my second season of hockey at Samwell...

Eric Bittle @omgcheckplease · Thu, Apr 9, 2015 | 11:07 PM

#OneMoreGame

Eric Bittle @omgcheckplease · Sun, Apr 12, 2015 | 8:22 PM

home.

Eric Bittle @omgcheckplease · Sat, Apr 18, 2015 | 8:33 AM

do you ever call your mama first thing in the morning because the ancient oven in your sport team's Haus is on the fritz lol

Eric Bittle @omgcheckplease · Sat, Apr 18, 2015 | 8:39 AM

I'm on the ground with my forehead against this oven's door

Eric Bittle @omgcheckplease · Sat, Apr 18, 2015 | 8:42 AM

Jack: ...did something happen
Me: betsy's not well
Jack: oh. is that. . . an aunt

Eric Bittle @omgcheckplease · Sat, Apr 18, 2015 | 10:34 AM

Waiting outside of Dex's class to tell him everything again but in person for the third time.

Eric Bittle @omgcheckplease · Sat, Apr 18, 2015 | 12:04 PM

Dex: have you ever considered baking less?
Me: I don't understand your question?

Eric Bittle @omgcheckplease · Sat, Apr 18, 2015 | 11:08 PM

pies baked today: 0

Eric Bittle @omgcheckplease · Sat, Apr 18, 2015 | 11:11 PM

Sometimes the things you love in your life just go away. You just have to take a deep breath and keep going.

Eric Bittle @omgcheckplease · Sat, Apr 18, 2015 | 11:18 PM

Well, congrats to Jack Zimmermann for signing. It's official...

Eric Bittle @omgcheckplease · Sun, Apr 19, 2015 | 8:17 AM

Another Samwell morning. Jack and Shitty are across the hall talking about Dibs...

Eric Bittle @omgcheckplease · Sun, Apr 19, 2015 | 1:52 PM

I got one batch of cookies done, but B. shut off halfway through the second. *sigh*

Eric Bittle @omgcheckplease · Sun, Apr 19, 2015 | 5:10 PM

Trying to pay for my own froyo at Superberry but this boy: "It's on me, Bittle. I think I'm good for it."

Eric Bittle @omgcheckplease · Sun, Apr 19, 2015 | 5:11 PM

my mother has sent me at least 5 articles about jack signing

Eric Bittle @omgcheckplease · Sat, Apr 25, 2015 | 6:54 PM

Bittle and Shitty #SpringC

Eric Bittle @omgcheckplease · Mon, May 4, 2015 | 3:17 PM

Holster and Ransom both just texted me to see if I had lunch plans tomorrow. Separately...Something's fishy.

Eric Bittle @omgcheckplease · Mon, May 4, 2015 | 3:31 PM

SMH Group Text:
Me: I love y'all but no festive baking, please. The oven's fragile. Thx!
Holster: Wouldn't worry bout that!

Eric Bittle @omgcheckplease · Mon, May 4, 2015 | 10:59 PM

Things I Should Be Doing: studying for a final tomorrow
Things I Should Not Be Doing: thinking about tres leches

Eric Bittle @omgcheckplease · Tue, May 5, 2015 | 7:55 AM

Woke up to birthday wishes from #MamaBittle. Lovely AM phone call. What more could a boy ask for? (^_^)

Eric Bittle @omgcheckplease · Tue, May 5, 2015 | 8:04 AM

Lardo was at my door with a party horn! "Put on pants and get breakfast with me, grandpa."

Eric Bittle @omgcheckplease · Tue, May 5, 2015 | 8:05 AM

Lardo: You're so OOOOLD!
Me: I'm ancienntttt!!!

Eric Bittle @omgcheckplease · Tue, May 5, 2015 | 9:22 AM

HM. So I guess I won't be heading back to the Haus anytime soon.

Eric Bittle @omgcheckplease · Tue, May 5, 2015 | 9:28 AM

Lardo won't let me go back to get my notes for my final. "How do they look like? Jack can bring them." (ALL OF THEM ARE IN ON THIS!!!)

Eric Bittle @omgcheckplease · Tue, May 5, 2015 | 9:32 AM

WHAT IF THEY'RE THROWING AWAY THAT FILTHY COUCH!!!!!! #GOTYOURBACK #SAMWELLMENSHOCKEY #TRUEBROS #MYONLYWISH

Eric Bittle @omgcheckplease · Tue, May 5, 2015 | 9:52 AM

Me: I know y'all are up to something.
Jack: What?
Me: For my birthday!
Jack:...today's your birthday?
:(

Eric Bittle @omgcheckplease · Tue, May 5, 2015 | 1:14 PM

Well, that final went exactly as planned...And seriously???? Ransom and Holster are waiting outside. I think I'm being escorted.

Eric Bittle @omgcheckplease · Tue, May 5, 2015 | 1:22 PM

Me: I'm not gonna head back to the Haus.
Holster: What? We're here to grab lunch with you!
Me: Let's have lunch at the Haus
Rans: Nice try.

Eric Bittle @omgcheckplease · Tue, May 5, 2015 | 2:38 PM

Lord, how long does it take to move in a couch?...Maybe they're burning the old one...But they'd invite me! Hm. :/

Eric Bittle @omgcheckplease · Tue, May 5, 2015 | 4:06 PM

Does EVERYONE at Samwell know??? I'm being told that I'm allowed to tweet one more thing. And now—

Eric Bittle @omgcheckplease · Tue, May 5, 2015 | 5:17 PM

Testing. Testing. cool

Eric Bittle @omgcheckplease · Tue, May 5, 2015 | 5:19 PM

Hey, everyone! I'm Derek, number 28 for Samwell men's hockey team. I was given instructions to tweet for your favorite vlogger Eric Bittle.

Eric Bittle @omgcheckplease · Tue, May 5, 2015 | 5:20 PM

Bitty says "Don't you wreck my reputation." We're heading back to the Haus! Bittle says "I knew y'all were up to something."

Eric Bittle @omgcheckplease · Tue, May 5, 2015 | 5:22 PM

He totally didn't. About a minute away from the Haus! Unsuspecting Bittle...

Eric Bittle @omgcheckplease · Tue, May 5, 2015 | 5:37 PM

Bitty says "K, y'all. The whole team's here and I haven't baked anything. It's a surprise party. I get it."

Eric Bittle @omgcheckplease · Tue, May 5, 2015 | 5:37 PM

Bitty says "Aren't y'all gonna yell surprise?" He just saw it.

Eric Bittle @omgcheckplease · Tue, May 5, 2015 | 6:26 PM

(Sorry things got kegstery really fast.) Also Bitty probably wouldn't want photos of him crying posted all over the internet.

Eric Bittle @omgcheckplease · Tue, May 5, 2015 | 6:29 PM

Bitty is still crying. "I need to bake something right this second!"

Eric Bittle @omgcheckplease · Tue, May 5, 2015 | 6:32 PM

stop crying first —jack

Eric Bittle @omgcheckplease · Tue, May 5, 2015 | 6:34 PM
He wants his phone back. It was fun! If you're a Wellie, come over for the festivitiesssss. (My name's Derek.)

Eric Bittle @omgcheckplease · Thu, May 7, 2015 | 8:46 PM
Newsflash: I've been baking a lot. :) Jack's chirp of the day: "If we move the kitchen table out, you can bring your bed in." #VeryFunnyMrZimmermann #HarHar

Eric Bittle @omgcheckplease · Fri, May 8, 2015 | 12:57 PM
Well, Jack and Shitty just picked up their graduation robes.

Eric Bittle @omgcheckplease · Sun, May 17, 2015 | 7:42 AM
Class Day! #Samwell2015

Eric Bittle @omgcheckplease · Sun, May 17, 2015 | 10:42 AM
Jack: Hey, nice robes.
Shitty: Nice robes yourself, brother.

Eric Bittle @omgcheckplease · Sun, May 17, 2015 | 12:13 PM
As Rans explained to me "class day is fun & everyone wears cool hats, commencement is boring but you get to throw your hat at the end."

Eric Bittle @omgcheckplease · Sun, May 17, 2015 | 1:27 PM
They set up a few screens around the Quad. Jack and Shitty showed up on one and we made SO MUCH NOISE. Sorry to anyone here! #Samwell2015

Eric Bittle @omgcheckplease · Sun, May 17, 2015 | 1:57 PM
I'm already thinking of how I'll trick out my mortarboard in a few years. Detachable felt pie slice? Or should I go full helmet like Jack...

Eric Bittle @omgcheckplease · Sun, May 17, 2015 | 2:14 PM
Announcing awards for graduating seniors. #Samwell2015

Eric Bittle @omgcheckplease · Sun, May 17, 2015 | 2:32 PM
OH!! "For an unprecedented three years of captaincy and exhibiting outstanding character on and off the field of play." Jack!!

Eric Bittle @omgcheckplease · Sun, May 17, 2015 | 2:37 PM

Samwell 2015's Best Male Athlete! #GotYourBack #Samwoll2015

Eric Bittle @omgcheckplease · Sun, May 17, 2015 | 3:52 PM

~Seniors~shitty: so what are we gonna put in your "I Won Samwell" shiny trophy bowl

Eric Bittle @omgcheckplease · Mon, May 18, 2015 | 10:10 AM

Don't know how many times I've said to myself "Keep it together, Bittle." It doesn't seem to be working.

Eric Bittle @omgcheckplease · Mon, May 18, 2015 | 1:27 PM

This boy.

Eric Bittle @omgcheckplease · Fri, Jul 3, 2015 | 3:05 PM

Just in time for the festivities. :)

I LOVE GRAPHIC NOVELS!

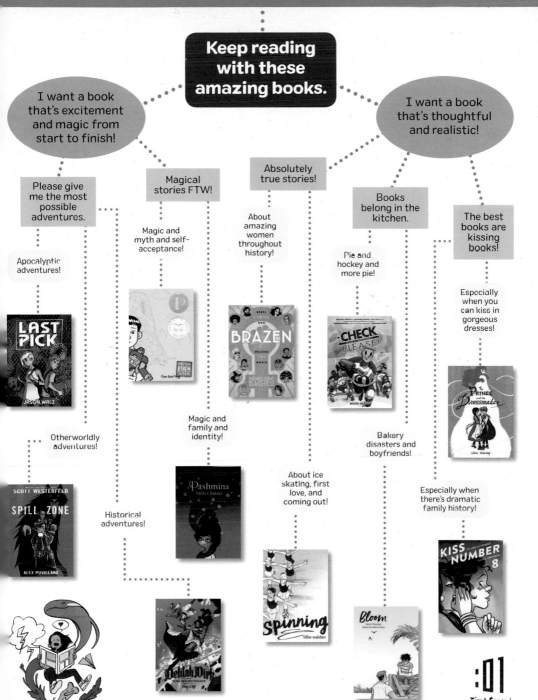

Keep reading with these amazing books.

I want a book that's excitement and magic from start to finish!

Please give me the most possible adventures.

Apocalyptic adventures!

LAST PICK
JASON WALZ

Otherworldly adventures!

SCOTT WESTERFELD
SPILL ZONE
ALEX PUVILLAND

Magical stories FTW!

Magic and myth and self-acceptance!

Magic and family and identity!

Pashmina
Nidhi Chanani

Historical adventures!

Delilah Dirk
Tony Cliff

Absolutely true stories!

About amazing women throughout history!

BRAZEN
PENELOPE BAGIEU

About ice skating, first love, and coming out!

Spinning
tillie walden

I want a book that's thoughtful and realistic!

Books belong in the kitchen.

Pie and hockey and more pie!

CHECK, PLEASE!

Bakery disasters and boyfriends!

Bloom

The best books are kissing books!

Especially when you can kiss in gorgeous dresses!

The Prince and the Dressmaker
Jen Wang

Especially when there's dramatic family history!

KISS NUMBER 8

:01
First Second

First Second

Copyright © 2018 by Ngozi Ukazu
Published by First Second
First Second is an imprint of Roaring Brook Press,
a division of Holtzbrinck Publishing Holdings Limited Partnership
175 Fifth Avenue, New York, NY 10010

Library of Congress Control Number: 2017957140

Hardcover ISBN: 978-1-250-17795-7
Paperback ISBN: 978-1-250-17796-4

Our books may be purchased in bulk for promotional, educational, or business use.
Please contact your local bookseller or the Macmillan Corporate and Premium Sales Department
at (800) 221-7945 ext. 5442 or by e-mail at MacmillanSpecialMarkets@macmillan.com.

First edition, 2018
Special thanks to Chelle Finkler
Edited by Calista Brill and Kiara Valdez
Book design by Andrew Arnold and Molly Johanson
Printed in China

Paperback: 1 3 5 7 9 10 8 6 4 2
Hardcover: 1 3 5 7 9 10 8 6 4 2